AF447662

POP FLY KISS

An Alpha Male Curvy Woman Romance

SAVANNAH KOLE

Copyright © 2020 by Savannah Kole

All rights reserved.

Book Cover Designed by Ardent Artist Books

No part of this book may be reproduced in any form or by any electronic or mechanical means, including information storage and retrieval systems, without written permission from the author, except for the use of brief quotations in a book review.

Published by
Ardent Artist Books
ardentartistbooks.com

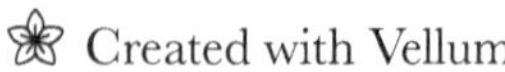 Created with Vellum

Contents

Chapter One

TACOMA, WASHINGTON

"Jared darling! Wakey! Wakey! It's a beautiful day to rise and win, baby."

It was his mother's voice, sharp and shrilling, it was over the top, which was what she had intended.

He desperately wanted to howl back at her to make her stop just before she started her morning chorus, but he had to be the gentleman. The perfect gentleman, never to lose his temper, heads up, shoulders high, chin straight, calm voice deepened with masculinity and utmost control of everything else around him.

He had learned all that growing up as a kid; one

of the many lessons alongside how to brush his teeth was that *as a man, you're never to be seen afraid or caught dead whimpering* he took that lesson so seriously that even when his HOW TO BE A MAN tutor and father, Mr. Rex Somner died, he stood with his chin up even higher than ever before. He was terrified at nine years old but he wouldn't fret. He owed it to be loyal to the memory of his father and of course to keep his Mom safe and happy.

So every morning when Mrs. Somner's screeching voice attempted to damage his eardrums as well as his ego, he held himself calm and maintained his composure.

"Honeycomb, sugar plum…" Her voice started again but this time it sounded more deliberate and to annoy him further with an endearing chant.

Jared understood the signals and stormed outside his bedroom door, he announced his arrival by joining her chant, "Mom, you're my sweetie pie. Oh my Cuppy cake—now I'm awake…"

While remixing the lyrics to suit his own purpose, she wouldn't stop until she was satisfied, and as he watched her impatiently waiting for him to stop singing so that he could kiss her good morning, he couldn't help the snippy look on his face.

Watching her close her mouth at last, smile with loving eyes, Jared planted a kiss on both her cheeks but noticed a bit of hesitation from her.

"You know better than to stop me in mid-song," she concluded, wanting to make sure she still had her hedges in place.

"Mom…" He protested against her.

"No buts, darling, do I make myself clear?" She asked again, only this time he knew this little routine could easily turn into a full-fledge drama and he'd have a weeping adult in his bosom that needed reassuring all day long. To save himself from long-term costs, he simply conceded, "Yes, Ma'am, I hear you."

"Good! That's my pumpkin," she said, pulling at his chin and going another round to piss him off.

But instead of taking it personal, Jared drew her into his warm embrace and planted a kiss on her head again before allowing his chin to sit comfortably over her head showing how much he had grown over the years. "Love you, mom."

She wiggled out of his embrace and then slapped his shoulders, "Now we're done talking, have a seat for your breakfast, I made your favorite; toast and cheese, serve your tea or coffee, whatever you want with it." She had rambled all through the hallway into the kitchen where Jared beat her and was now seated for breakfast.

As he munched on a piece of toast, he started talking again, "Thanks Mom, you shouldn't have."

"Totally, son," she said, with a tone of finality.

AS HE TOSSED over in his twin-sized bed, holding fast to the bunk to keep himself from falling off, he discovered that it was all a dream. The morning *song*, the *toast*, the *kisses and hugs* and his *Mom*. He didn't have any of that right now, all there was, was him on the upper bunk closer to the ceiling fan and the fearful sound it made.

He missed his Mom, *a lot*. He was just beginning to adopt without her, practically a thousand miles away. Waking up daily was different for him here and he couldn't imagine how it felt for his Mom.

Understanding that his absence from home felt like a loss and that it was going to take some time for her to adjust too, but he had his own dreams to pursue now, and he couldn't let a thing hold him back.

When he left for the Memphis Redbirds, the

Triple-A ball team for the St. Louis Cardinals about a year ago, she wasn't ready to be without the charming face she rose to every morning. All these years they had spent as mother and son, the only night they did spend apart from each other was the night his Dad died. Ever since, they'd stayed glued together, his mother, a widow and single parent—he almost didn't want to go! But it was a chance of a lifetime, Major League Baseball—all boys dreamt of becoming a professional baseball player—and Jared Somner was no different.

His mother was the one who had advised him to start playing and when he got good at it, he couldn't help but revel in the opportunities he now had. Scouts, agents, even a call from the St. Louis G-M. Jared was on his way…

NOW WIDE AWAKE from his dream, he laid there still reminiscing over the last conversation they had while he was preparing to leave home. He had promised her so much and those promises kept him going most of the time.

"Hey—hey, Mom, look here, I'm doing this for us remember?" He had said leaning closer over the table and

touching her hands but she only snorted noisily and wouldn't look at him. "Okay, fine, I agree I'm doing this typically for me and for my own selfish-interests, but you taught me to pursue my dreams and I've been doing you proud so far, so be happy for me."

She glanced at him with tears in her eyes. She shook her head.

Jared squeezed her hand harder, "You know every player's dream is to get called up to the majors and I made it, Mom. I don't want to miss this because I'm going to take care of you…"

"Honey, I know all that, I'm just a little worried about you. It's just that I'm not used to not having you around," she confessed, standing up to clear the plates they ate off of.

"I'm going to make you proud, Mom."

"I'm worried about you—I don't want you to be lonely," she said, clanking the dishes in the sink.

Jared let go a snort, "Mom, there's groupies everywhere! I won't be lonely."

His mother turned around and shook her head at him, "I'm not talking about that. One day, you're gonna wake up and want a girl to stay."

"No, I won't," Jared cockily rejoined.

His mother let go a laugh, "Just you wait! Some girl's smile is gonna knock you on your ass and you'll never know what hit you."

Jared laughed out loud, "You're my girl, Mom. And besides, I won't allow that to happen."

His mother shook her head, "You'll see. But when you do son, I'd like to meet her."

Jared just grinned, "Yea, sure."

Chapter Two

She is going to avoid me, right?
Of course, she should avoid me
I really don't have time to spare babysitting a
heartbroken adult
If she talks to me I'll just avoid her and look
straight ahead

Memphis Redbirds Training Camp

Jared's thoughts rampaged through his head as he got ready to leave his hotel room which he shared with three other players. He had broke it off with one of his groupies just in time for the next game. Actually, they had been together for a game previously and finding her here again wasn't cool. She had travelled from Arizona to Tennessee just to see him again. His fear was that she might want to get back with him, but Jared just wanted something new and that wasn't *her*.

Leaving his room with his hotel mates, they made it to the stadium, unscathed. As they got down from the bus that had picked them up from the hotel, the groupies in their own bus had just arrived too.

And there was Kate.

The girl he had been dreading.

"Hello, Jared."

He was taken aback with her voice right behind him as he tried to get his backpack from the storage compartment. "Hey, what's up?" Jared asked, still not looking straight at her.

"How was your weekend? And training?" Kate asked, trying to push the conversation further.

He tried to avoid her, but she stuck like glue. "Hey, so…I'm done here, and you should be too," he said with a tone of finality, as he tapped her on the shoulder and swung his backpack behind him ready to storm off.

"But we're cool, right? Like, no one needs to know. You know, …" She stood there stammering, as Jared walked away waving his hand a little above his head before he faded away from her eyes.

AFTER PRACTICE and back in their hotel room, Jared had just gotten back from taken a shower. Dennis Caufield, one of his teammates, came in and made an announcement which wasn't exactly what he wanted to hear.

"Hey Jared, is it really over with Kate? Are you done with her *now*? Do you think I can have her?"

He kept on talking and wouldn't keep his mouth shut—then the whole room got involved. When they found out what it was about, they started cheering Jared on for his swift Casanova skills. By the way, Kate was one of the hottest groupies there was, and the boys had been discussing it secretly between them while he was in the bathroom.

"So, who's next Jared if it's no longer Kate?" Marco Avila asked, another one of his teammates.

He honestly had no one in mind and so he had no answer. "I'm laying off chicks for a while," he relayed with so much assertion as he knew that the groupies only needed a few days to settle in before they started to hover around again. It was an endless cycle.

But his teammates were not done, they started up again about the hottest groupies and asked him to make a choice. Most of them he didn't know yet, but it was fun following the names with jests until they got to the very last name.

"Sarah Millston!"

"Kate's friend? I'll pass," he answered. The unspoken rule was to avoid girls in the same groupie herd.

The whole room burst into laughter.

Jared was done making jokes about other people, he was on his way out of the room thinking it was all finished when someone suggested another name…

"Nicole Monroe? Have you seen her ass?" Dennis remarked, cupping his hands, grabbing at air.

"Oh, she's hot! Yeah, I've seen her. She hangs with a new group," Marco added.

"So, they're new to the Redbirds?" Jared asked, interested now.

"Yeah, think so. How about Penny Lawton?" Dennis quipped, holding his hand over his mouth trying to prevent himself from bursting out in laughter.

Nice name, but Jared had never heard or seen her before. So he wanted to evade the question but the guys wouldn't let him off the hook. Jared shrugged his shoulders.

"Frumpy Penny?" Dennis guffawed. "She hangs with Nicole and Maria?"

"Who's Maria?" Jared asked, still interested.

Marco chimed in now, "Maria Fernandez. She's hot too, and I would tap that, but my girl at home would know."

Jared now laughed, "How would she know? She's like a million miles away."

Marco agreed, but then relented, "I would know."

Jared secretly agreed and swallowed his acceptance of Marco's loyalty. "Penny? Is she cute?"

Marco and Dennis both burst out laughing again.

"No, just call her *Porky Penny* or *Plump Penny!*" Marco said, trying to contain his chortling.

Was she really that bad? Jared thought. "Why call her that?"

Dennis snorted, "Dude, have you seen her? She's like a BIG girl!"

Marco continued laughing too, "I think Badwell's already hooked up with her."

Jared didn't think it was funny. "Who here has slept with her?" Jared gazed around the room, but no one could claim the deed. "Then why call her fat? I mean, is she?"

"Wait till you see her," Dennis quickly replied.

Chapter Three

AUTOZONE PARK

I n her circle of friends, there were two types of girls; the ones who simply fantasized about the baseball players and the ones who targeted them for sport. Some people may want to call the latter *whores* but they were all *groupies*, and baseball player fanatics.

Penny Lawton was a blend of both. She was an awesome person, a baseball fan through and through, but her physique did not exactly portray her in the right light. **Plump Penny** was the pet name the players often called her, and well, you know the other names that she never got to hear in person.

.   .   .

"OHMIGOD! IT'S JARED SOMNER!"

"Where is he?" Penny asked excitedly as she walked along the aisle leading to the diamond with her friends. Each of them had a celebrity crush on at least one of the minor league players, while most of them were simply *Team Jared* despite knowing that he was out of their league.

"Penny, he isn't looking *your* way so quit straightening out that skirt, there are no curves." Her friend, Nicole chastised to the amusement of her own self-esteem.

"Y'all should quit the chubby girl dream, I'm curvy," Penny said, correcting them.

"Actually, Penny is curvier than any one of us here. Just look at her ass, so I am in support of her this time," Maria declared, which made the girls begin to stare at her backside in admiration, and jesting.

"So much for change and development," Nicole smirked at her.

They had been baseball groupies for three years straight, and had particularly formed a threesome —Penny, Nicole, and Maria. In all her years of being a groupie, only once had she had a player to herself; and regretted every minute of it. It was her first attempt at trying to bed one of them. She was drunk, he was high, and the act was sloppy, fast and unmemorable. *In fact, did it even happen?* It did, and they were an item for a hot minute.

Truth be told, there were dozens of little groupies like hers, and getting even remotely close was a task in itself. Since there were so many to choose from, the baseball players were particular, and usually chose from the pick of the litter.

As if the girls were reading her mind, Maria started laughing out loud as she reminisced over Penny's early relationship with Owen Badwell, center field.

"A penny for your thoughts," Nicole said teasingly, as she could already guess what was going on inside her head.

"Penny, you remember Owen? Your first love," Maria asked, pointing out towards center field.

It wasn't a topic she liked to discuss. It had been a very embarrassing one for her and what was worse was that she was forewarned. Owen was not the perfect or ideal boyfriend, but she convinced herself that it was okay to be in love with someone who wasn't perfect. And besides, Nicole and Maria only knew what they could see—or what Penny divulged—and not the real truth, that her experience with Owen was a foul one. It was all fun and games when they started dating after sex, but just days after, it turned into a total mess. Owen was bad at conversation and he was a sexual pervert; which would have been fun only that he was more of a talker without much action. He was a terrible kisser too. And when Owen spread the rumor that Penny was an *easy lay* and *good for head* she nearly lost it. Well, she had more self-esteem than that! So she dumped his ass.

Ever since, all she's wanted was to *feel* wanted … so the search began again. "Yes, I remember," she answered them in a devastated manner.

"Ohmigawd," Nicole exclaimed, as Penny whipped her head around to see what Nicole was hooting about.

Two other circles of groupies were hanging around the fences as well. Pretty, tall, thin— gorgeous. *How was she to compete with them?*

"Do we know any of them?" Penny asked, honestly.

Maria eyed the other girls from head to toe, "Nah, yah, well—maybe that girl with the pig-tails. I think her name is Kate."

Nicole eyed the girl in pig-tails. "Yea, her name is Kate. I heard she and Jared were a thing for like two-seconds."

Penny watched from afar as the herd of girls flittered from one fence to the other, and cheered with a piercing scream each and every time a ball player hit a ball high in the air. It didn't matter to them whether it was a fly ball or a line drive, all they cared about was the way the ball player looked in his uniform.

"Jared Somner is up next," Maria noted, walking closer to the fence to get a better look.

The two other girls tagged along. Nicole stuck her nose through the fence, while Penny hung the iron with both hands.

Behind the fence, Jared reached the diamond and began his turn at batting practice. The first pitch he let pass—too low. The second pitch was just right, and Jared swung for center field. Penny and the other girls all watched the baseball soar high and far as it sailed across and above Owen Badwell's raised glove, and over the center field back wall.

Penny smiled inwardly. *Serves that asshole right— shouldn't have been picking his nose.*

The girls all watched Jared run around the bases, then hit home and then did the oddest thing. Ran straight towards them!

With their eyes bugged out, Nicole, Maria and Penny all watched Jared as he jogged towards their locale of the fence. *What the heck?*

"Haven't seen you three around—did you catch my homer?" Jared asked, gazing at Nicole first.

Attractive, blond Nicole smiled seductively, "Of course, how could we miss it?"

Then Jared cocked his head towards Maria. A Latin beauty, Maria too smiled suggestively. "What did you think?"

Maria winked at him, "You're the best there is Jared."

Then Jared rested eyes on Penny. *Crashing into Penny* was more like it and Jared dropped his eyes down the length of her. *Fat? Where?* There was something strange about her…"And you? Did you see my homer over center field?"

Penny's smiled dropped at the sight of him. Jared Somner was *hotter* than *hot*. He was drop-dead gorgeous! Brown hair, heavenly brown eyes, straight white teeth—*damn he was gonna sell a lot of breakfast cereals,* she thought. "You could have gotten several more feet if you had bent your elbow more," Penny said, watching the air go out of his balloon.

Jared stared at her for a moment like she had three eyes in the center of her head. He squinted his eyes at her once, then turned around and jogged back to practice.

Chapter Four

MEMPHIS REDBIRDS VS. ROUND ROCK EXPRESS

*O*h *shit…*, Penny thought.

Settling down in the benches now, Penny took a seat to get the best view of everything happening on the field. She didn't want to miss even the slightest detail of the game.

She was drunk on Jared Somner.

Odd that he grew quiet after her comment about his elbow being too high. Well, it *was* too high. She had been watching baseball since she was old enough to understand. Her three older brothers and father were all baseball fans—and season ticket holders for the Cardinals. She knew what to look for. *But damn her big mouth!*

Sitting high and up above the other two girls, Penny had a good birds-eye view of all the circle of groupies all in attendance. Kate, plus her friends and another group of girls all giggling and pointing away at the players. Penny too, couldn't help but gaze out towards Jared, at third. He was busy concentrating on a Round Rock player at bat.

Meanwhile, Maria was definitely rooting for Marco Avila to make the most waves. She cheered him on and cussed at anyone that seemed like an obstruction to his victory on the field. Marco had been her target to bed for a few weeks now.

As the game went on, Penny overheard the other groupies share stories about the players they had sex with, and who was better in bed. Penny listened to the stories half-heartedly, and at seldom points, she laughed at their snide remarks. It was advantageous for her to know beforehand who was terrible at romance so that she could avoid the bad blood. She desperately needed to prevent history from repeating itself and inadvertently looked out at Owen in center field.

But each of the stories only gave more validation to her secret admiration of Jared. He was the perfect guy, according to a few. Handsome and attractive. His body was built like that of a sports model. She imagined how much stamina he had. He would sweep her off her feet with ease and scoop her into his arms for some time before seeking any support from a wall or chair.

He was also one of the best Triple-A ballplayers she had seen lately. She had read online that he had been scouted often, and that there were rumors that he might be called up soon to play for the Cardinals. He had a lot of talent, both on and off the field. He was known as a player, *literally*, and according to Jennifer in herd two, *the biggest dick she's had in a long time*.

By nature, she didn't want to appreciate knowing he had a huge dick—but there it was—hanging in front of her. *It must be difficult for him really,* Penny thought, as she gazed over at third base again. To be blessed with a body for sin, after all, why have just one flavor of ice cream when you can have variety? *How else will the rest of us get close enough to all of his awesomeness if he were loyal?* She paused and took another glance at Jared—only this time, he had been gazing up at the stands. *Who was he searching for?* It seemed like he took his sweet time too, glancing over all the patrons in the benches. *Who was so important? He really needed to concentrate on the ball game.*

It was hard to explain what had happened next, but the small ball had flown off the field and landed somewhere among the spectators. It wasn't an unusual incidence, and the fly ball hit Penny right smack on her shoulder.

Nicole and Maria both sprung from their seats and ran towards Penny's plight.

"Ohmigod, are you all right?"

"That must of fuckin' hurt!"

AS SHE LOOKED at herself in the mirror in the Redbird's convenience room, she was almost sure that something was inherently wrong. The odds of being the one who gets hit by a foul ball must be considerably high. *Why her?!*

A stadium worker was kind enough to bring her a bag of ice so that she could place it against the throbbing. She had been leaning up against a brick wall with the icepack against her shoulder when she overheard two girls talking just outside the wall near the girls bathroom. They didn't see her standing there.

"He asked me to meet him after the game," one of the girls chirped.

"Gawd, you're so lucky, you think you're gonna suck his dick tonight?" The other girl trilled.

"I dunno, maybe. You think I should play hard to get? Or should I just—you know—give in?"

Penny rolled her eyes. The urge to leave the stadium was strong. But she didn't. She had to wait for Nicole and Maria and the end of the game. It had been bottom of the ninth—it wouldn't be long now.

Her pain was intensifying, and she shirked by its throbbing. The ice wasn't helping, only making her numb.

She couldn't take much more of this agonizing wait for the game to end.

And then, it did.

The cheers from the stands overwhelmed the halls and the convenience area. The Redbirds won. *Yeah...*

Penny peeked outside the open door and watched as hundreds of fans exited the stands. She waited anxiously for her friends to appear, but they hadn't arrived. Only the same stadium worker who came by to check on her.

"You okay? You need more ice?"

Penny practically had tears in her eyes, the pain was so dreadfully bad. She nodded her head, yes and watched the worker disappear behind the crowd.

Penny closed her eyes and wiped a tear away that rolled down her cheek. *Nicole and Maria probably caught ball players,* she thought, shaking her head and reopening her eyes.

Focusing once, she nearly passed out. *What the heck? Was she dreaming?*

"Thought that was you," he said, reaching for her, but not touching her shoulder.

Penny could not believe he was actually concerned over her well-being! "The hazard of being a fan."

Jared smiled, and then actually took the icepack away from her shoulder to inspect her wound.

Her bare shoulder was **purple**, bruising.

Jared gave her a reassuring smile, "Not so bad. Keep the ice on it for a few hours."

Penny swallowed her own grin, his presence was overwhelming. His body so close to hers caused her to shiver. She nodded her head.

Jared stuck his thumb out. "Gotta go."

And he was off in a cloud of smoke…

Never to be seen again.

Maybe it was a dream … or wishful thinking.

Chapter Five

AUTOZONE PARK

The Following Day

The threesome were back at the ballpark watching another practice. The two other groupie herds were there too.

With her arm now in a sling, Penny sat with her two friends listening to them go on and on comparing their escapades with two random ball players.

"I can't believe he asked me to do it in his car," Nicole relayed, munching on some popcorn.

"Well, you're the idiot who went in his backseat," Maria shot back, gazing around the field for Marco Avila. She won't admit to it, but she once did in the backseat of a Ford Pinto (Google that).

"Thank God I was wearing a skirt this time," Nicole continued, crunching on the corn. "There wasn't much room back there to get my jeans off!"

"We went back to his hotel room," Maria gushed.

Penny swallowed her grin. After swallowing a bunch of pain medications, she finally felt comfortable enough to at least get some rest. Nicole had gone home with the first baseman, Dennis Caufield. A player she had been after for weeks now. *Let's see how long she could keep his interest.* And Maria slept with the third baseman…? *Unsure about his name…*

"Shush!" Maria suddenly exclaimed, grabbing Nicole by the arm. "Incoming."

Penny looked over to see Dennis and Jared walking towards them. Both of them with baseball bats in their hands.

Nicole beamed and instantly looked at Dennis, who shyly looked down at the ground.

"Hey," he said to her, digging his bat into the grass.

"Hey yourself," she replied, biting down on her lower lip.

Jared glanced once at Maria, but then rested eyes on Penny. "How's the shoulder?"

Penny looked up at him but instantly looked away and eyed the other herds all looking over and pointing. "Medication helps."

Jared smiled, "I bet."

Penny then watched as Dennis and Nicole walked away from the threesome to talk. Jared looked back at Penny again, ignored Maria who by this time, had been desperately trying to gain his attention.

Hair flip. Check.

Cleavage. Check.

Licking lower lip. Pass…

"Are you doing anything tonight?" Jared asked Penny.

Penny looked at him like HE had three eyes in the center of HIS head. "You mean after the game?"

"Yea, after the game," he repeated, swinging the bat around on his left side.

Penny's heart began to thump hard. She swore he could see it through her blouse. "No, I don't have any plans."

Jared let go a half-grin, "Great, stay here in the stands, I'll meet you after the game."

And then he was off in another cloud of smoke.

Twirling the bat around in his hand like some poker-chip.

Did she just agree to meet Jared Somner after the game?

Before she could do anything, Maria grabbed at her hand. "What the fuck was that? Did Jared Somner just ask you out on a date?"

Penny nodded her head, no. "I think he feels sorry for me."

"Why?" Maria asked, alarmed.

"Cause I got hit by a foul ball," Penny affirmed, looking out towards his locale.

Jared wasn't paying any attention to her now. He was busy conversing with his teammates out on the field.

"WHAT THE FUCK WAS THAT? Did Jared Somner just ask Penny Lawton out on a date?"

"Guess Jared must be tired from grinding hard," Dennis remarked, stretching out his calves.

Jared ignored his friends who kept on razzing him.

"Plump Penny? Really man?" Dennis asked, trying to push him over the edge.

"Leave it alone," Jared finally warned him.

"What do you see in her?" Andy Ackerman, another teammate randomly asked.

Jared shook his head. He honestly didn't know. He didn't see *anything* in her, other than the fact that her statement bothered him. All he really wanted was to talk to her. "Nothing," he ended up saying.

"Pity date!" Dennis roared, so the guys who were near could hear. "We've got ourselves a pity date!"

"Pity date? Who?" Marco asked, running over excited.

Dennis pushed Marco's chest, "Jared..."

"With who?" Marco asked again, looking over at Jared.

"Plump Penny," Dennis laughed.

Marco began to join in. "No shit, really? Pity date, cause she got hit?"

Jared shook his head, "You're all morons—let's warm up."

Chapter Six

After the Game

Jared walked away from the field and began looking around at the stands and in the direction of where Penny usually sat down during the games, but she wasn't there. The lump in his throat was unfamiliar to him, so he shrugged it off.

Walking back towards the locker room, he looked down at his cleats in defeat. What the heck was happening to him? How could a simple statement cause so much damage? *His elbow was too high? Really? Last night, he tossed and turned just thinking about it. Was his elbow really that high in his swing? What could he do better? And why, oh why, was he hanging on this girls every word? Who was she anyway?*

A sleepless night suddenly morphed into some kind of obsession. Penny Lawton, whoever she was —was inside his head now! *How could he get rid of her?* **Girls and baseball do not mix**, isn't that what all coaches say? Hit and run—repeat—females were just a means to an end. End it, and soon. He was, but she wasn't sitting in the stands! *Where the fuck was she?*

BACK AT THE HOTEL, he lie in bed awake— another sleepless night. Both his roommates were gone for the evening—hook-ups, for sure. Dennis was probably with Nicole again, and Marco was probably with some—whomever, cheating on his girl back home—Jared didn't care anymore. The only thing he did care for was … *what?* Asking Penny why she thought his elbow was too high? Or, was it something else entirely? The more he thought about it, the more he realized it wasn't about any one question—no, it was *her*.

She intrigued him.

She was different.

He had heard the rumors that Owen spurted

out, but he had never listened to them. His mother taught him to never misjudge anyone by their appearance alone, and he never once entertained the idea of thinking of her as fat, porky, chubby or plump (as they usually called her). She was *pretty* to him. She had dark brown shoulder length hair and green eyes—were they green? No, they were *hazel*—as he concentrated harder. Beautiful browns and greens; a pert nose and pink lips—*oh shit,* as he slowly closed his eyes imagining himself running his lips across hers. And did he mention her breasts? *Oh fucking hell!* He thought again, as he crossed his legs, feeling his dick getting harder fantasizing about licking her nipples to no end. Rolling over in bed, he had expected her to show up at his hotel room like some kind of party favor, but sadly, she never did.

SO ON THE THIRD DAY—HE went a little bit insane. He had secretly waited for her in her usual spot by the fence, but when she didn't show up he hissed at the fact that she was deliberately avoiding him now and decided it was better to just concentrate on work.

Coming back with his head focused completely on his game (as he ought to have done from the very beginning) he went into the field and played with a certain kind of fury. Jared Somner was a great player on any given day, but on *this* day, his name rang more among the audience than it ever did before. Six for six—with stats through the roof! Three home-runs, two double's and a triple. He couldn't have asked for a better game!

But Penny wasn't there. She didn't get to watch.

He had been approached several times after the game to let off some stream by multiple groupies, but he turned them all down and decided to go for a run. Keeping in shape meant everything to him, and besides, it was better to *sweat* than to *agonize*.

He snapped out of his delusional reverie and looked down at his watch—>8:00PM

Pulling a black sweatshirt over his head, he wore black joggers and a pair of Nike running shoes. Grabbing his phone and ear pods, he looked across at his bed and wished Penny had been lying there.

Outside, a chilly breeze swept across his face and exposed hands, which he shoved in the pockets of his jacket. As he began to run, he thought about leaving her friends a note, or try calling or texting her, but in all honesty, he was *waiting on her to do so first.* Until now, all girls were coming to him! He never had to beg, never had to wait—girls had been lining up at his door…

All, but one in particular.

He wanted to call her, but something in him made jest of his flickering ego and he was stirred with anger. Then he began to curse under his breath praying that she had better have a decent reason for making him go through all this turmoil, so he picked up his phone to call, he remembered that he had not even saved her number decently; typical of him. He called the first time, it rang to no avail.

And then a second time, still there was no answer. He looked down at his watch again—
>8:30PM

Who the hell does she think she is? He convinced himself to try calling a third time—she answered, but the call seemed to have been ended abruptly from the other end.

Within the twinkle of an eye, he had felt so many different emotions all at once; fear, anger, worry, smashed ego, revenge, but mostly fear. He convinced himself that no woman on Earth at that moment had the guts to ignore his call even once, so it was a question of her safety. He was scared as terrifying thoughts engulfed his mind. He hastened his steps allowing the sole of his sneakers pound aggressively on the Earth with each step that he took.

His heartbeat was racing, from the night exercise and inhaling and exhaling of the chilly air but more from the worry in his heart that something may have happened to her. He wasn't sure where to look or even what to do when he found her, but he resolved not to fret until he had heard her voice and seen her face to face.

Chapter Seven

Heading towards the bar—his teammates usual hangout spot—he hastened his steps but on instinct, took to a different route than he would normally run through.

Not so long after the change in direction, he started to hear shrilling shouts, he headed towards the voice as it got more intense like a cry for help, then the voice stopped. He pulled his ear pods away from his ears to see if he had been wrong, but he wasn't. The cry for help got louder. Fear gripped him, he didn't mind not having a weapon or being on a lonely street, he ran faster towards the commotion and to his shock, he stumbled upon Owen Badwell … trying to force down … Penny?

"What the fuck?" His voice rang deep on anger

and disgust as he ran towards them.

Owen raised his hands in the air in defeat. "Dude, I didn't know she was your property. I was just looking for an easy fuck," he said, slurring his words.

Obviously drunk, Jared realized. Then he looked over at Penny and immediately stepped in front of her to shield her from any further harm. Jared lowered his eyes down the length of Owen. *Why was he even on the team?* He was worthless. Sub-standard batting average, mistakes, errors—it was only a matter of days when was he gonna be cut.

"Dude, she's an easy lay—let's both do her," Owen said, adding fuel to the fire.

Jared cocked his head, "Owen, I think you'd better leave."

Owen spat on the ground. "Dude, she's not worth it. She's fat, you'll see, it's hard to get your dick in."

Jared immediately grabbed him by his shirt and brought him into his face. "I wanna punch your lights out, you know that? But I don't want to ruin my chances of major league. That's the only thing holding me back of not *fucking you up* right now."

Owen gulped. Then raised his arms in the air in surrender. "Yea-yea—no dude, you're right. We'd both get thrown off the team. No chick is worth that."

Jared released his grip on him and then pushed his body away. Owen nearly tripped over on his own two left feet and braced himself from his face hitting the concrete.

Jared and Penny watched Owen walk away, then disappear through the trees on the other side of the street.

Jared then turned around and looked down at Penny. She was easily several inches shorter than he was and the realization hit him hard. He was also taken aback with thoughts raiding his mind; thoughts of *what if*, as she stood before him silently drowned in fear. He liked to see women scared and quivering before him but not in this manner. Not Penny, and not when the fear had not been instilled by him. From that moment, he just wanted to protect her, to keep her safe, to be there for her. He looked deep into her eyes. The hesitation was still there. "You okay?"

Penny gazed over across the street to make sure Owen was out of sight. "We were seeing each other for a few weeks," she stammered.

Jared swallowed hard, "Yeah, I know."

"He thought since I was easy back then ... that

I would be easy now," she confessed, looking down at the ground.

Jared gazed away. His heart pounded recklessly. In this moment, he so wanted to just take her in his arms. *Why couldn't he? What was holding him back?*

But then…

Penny lunged for his body and grabbed him into her, wrapping her arms around his backside. The feeling was so intense, it practically stole his breath away. "Thank you," she whispered into his chest.

He pulled her into him and held her near. "He's gone now, I won't let him hurt you."

Penny shook her head. Feeling him so close, she never wanted to let him go. "I know, it's just…" she said, pulling her head away from his body. "It's just I can't believe…"

Jared looked down into her eyes, "Can't believe what?"

Then Penny pushed his body away from hers. "I was a pity date?" Dennis had told Nicole and Nicole told her that she was a *pity date*. That's the real reason she didn't remain seated after the game that night. The *only reason* why she ignored his calls and tied her hands behind her back to *not* text him. She was chopped down that day, learning the truth, and the reality hit hard. She was convinced she was in love with him. After that day, the day he came to see how she was after she had been hit by the foul ball—it was the *concern* that hooked her in. He allowed her a glimpse of who he really was—a good person. Not some fantasized version of some far-away baseball hero, but the *real* Jared Somner— a worried human being. But then Dennis had told Nicole, and Nicole told her that she was a pity date. ***That stung.*** Hurt her heart to no end and she cried for hours. She wasn't going to allow a boy do that to her, she had already lived through a broken heart with Owen, she wasn't going to allow it to happen again!

Jared started to chuckle. "Pity date? Who told you that?"

Penny didn't think it very funny. "My friend Nicole."

Jared released his body away from hers and shoved his hands down the pockets of his jacket. "And Dennis told Nicole?"

"Yes," Penny said, biting down on her lower lip.

"Consider the source," Jared explained, shaking his head. Then silence.

An awkward stare.

A war of wills...

Chapter Eight

Trying to exert control over the rush of emotions running through his veins he tried to calm down his heart. He looked down at her and she had that look on her face, the one that always got him mesmerized.

Nobody said a word, they stared at each other as if waiting for the other to make the first move, Penny couldn't take the stare so she looked away from him.

It was as though, she had plunged a dagger into him at that moment, and he couldn't take much more. "Penny Lawson, what do you want?" He asked her fiercely. "What do you want from me?" He reiterated like she didn't hear him the first time.

She stood there dumbfounded at his

intimidating presence. This was the moment for her to speak, to say that she wanted to be *his* and him, *hers*. To say she wanted *everything*. Everything that there was to him but she was tongue-tied! She couldn't help herself; the way he looked at her at that moment was different, poles apart from every other time.

She allowed her lips to part but still no words, then he closed in on her, holding her hands. His simple reaction did her in. "I want to be with you … at least once," she slowly confessed.

Jared realized instantly that her groupie-fantasy was still in play. She was still just a groupie. But was she really? "Once?" He let go, disbelieving this was her one and only resolve. "And then you'll go away?"

Penny slowly closed her eyes. *Did she just agree to that?* Before she could debate it, she heard herself say, "Yes."

Jared shook his feelings off for her and let go a sigh. Exhausted from feeling intense emotions, he said, "Do you live nearby?"

SHE DID LIVE NEARBY. In fact, Nicole, Maria and her decided to move in together. Get a three bedroom apartment and split the rent. Penny knew that Maria was out of town that evening and Nicole was out with Dennis so the apartment would be empty for at least several hours.

It was tranquil, calm … ordinary, normal as they walked hand-in-hand through the living room and towards her bedroom. But once inside, a volcano erupted.

Jared slammed the door behind them and pushed her body up against the closure. It was a long-overdue kiss.

Their lips collided and her heartbeat tripled. She responded with so much agility, as the kiss got more intense, tongues stroking, his hands grabbed her waist tightly, leaning her towards the wood as he heightened the moment of his lips and strokes. His fingers got busy and his lips began to multitask all over her flesh.

His hands wandered from her waist up inside her jacket into her back, as he made sensitive marks along the middle while letting his lips alternate between her kiss and her shoulders, rendering a much-desired torture on her body.

As his fingers and lips went to work, he let out his left hand that had been holding onto her face, and was now on her neck holding her firmed in place as he pressed her body firmly to his so that she could feel his groins atop her waist. She was five-foot-three against his height that she had estimated to be at least six-two.

Her mind started wandering away as she struggled to keep up with the ferocity and maintain the kiss, she thought of letting her hands grab his groins from his joggers in a soft squeeze. She was about to and as though he had been reading her mind, he pulled back from her only to walk them backwards to lie on the bed.

Penny quickly began to pull up his sweatshirt, as he began to undress her down to her bra. Off went her jacket and shoes, and luckily she was wearing a dress that night and it came off in one big swoop. Pulling down his joggers, he exposed what was underneath—no underwear, and a trail of dark soft hair leading down to his swollen dick. Gasping for air, she threw her head back as Jared yanked down her bra-straps to expose her breasts and nipples to his thirsty mouth. Cupping his hand under one mound, he brought her flesh up to his lips and mouth, sucking hard and licking until she reached down and brought her hand around his enlarged penis. She simply had to stroke it—to measure the reality against the fantasy—and it did not disappoint. She couldn't wait to feel him inside of her.

Releasing his mouth from her breasts, he whispered, "I don't have a condom, do you?"

Yes! … *Yes,* she thought, she did keep condoms next to her bed. She had to! How else was she going to entice any guy to her bed? Convenience will win every time. She leaned over and opened up the drawer, pulled out one package and then quickly handed it over to him.

Jared smiled and then rolled off over her, opening the package with his teeth but before he could place the sheath over his penis, Penny pulled his hand away and began to suck on his erection. Closing his eyes, he whispered, "Oh fuck, you don't have to do that." And gently pulled her face away from his so that he could finish putting the condom on.

Rolling her back over, he spread her arms out wide above her head, and held her there with both his arms. Straddling over her midriff, he gazed down at her lying there, soaking in how beautiful she looked with her hair spread out against the pillow and the moonlight covering half her face. He leaned in and gave her a gentle kiss, all the while clutching her arms above her head. Kisses trailing down her neck, grazing towards the tips of her peaks and then spreading her legs apart with his knee, entering slowly so that her velvety walls could adjust to his girth. Leisurely pumping, he took his time and released his grip on her arms only to wrap his around her body in a warm embrace.

Penny enclosed him in return, showing him how much she loved him, relishing in his sole attention and trying to memorize every inch of him inside her. Slow, tepid thrusts quickly turned frenzied, as she thrust against his loins, inviting him deeper and deeper … until she heard his moan against her lips and she quickly felt herself bloom and extract into her own orgasm.

Chapter Nine

Breathing heavily, Jared remained on top of her, still not moving or quickly getting off like others before him had did. Penny thought it odd how he languidly remained in tact until he finally lifted up his head.

"That was amazing," he softly said against her cheek.

Penny gently ran her hand over his firm buttocks up to his lower back. "I know."

Jared looked down at her smiling. "I never knew it could be like this."

Penny didn't quite understand. Did she miss something? Could it be? "What do you mean?"

Jared ultimately pulled out and then rolled over to lie on his back. Pulling the condom off his limp penis, he quickly grabbed a tissue from the side desk then threw the condom perfectly in the waste basket in the corner of her room. Cropping his head up with his elbow he lied there naked, running his eyes down her nakedness. "With you silly."

Normally Penny would feel ashamed about her body and when the after glow would wear off, she would hurriedly get dressed. But with Jared, she did not feel ashamed, and ran her own hand down between her breasts, causing her nipples to rise from the touch.

Jared's eyes immediately focused on the reaction, and with his other hand began to trace around her breasts with simplicity.

Penny snickered, "I know you've probably been with a thousand girls by now, how can I be any different?"

Jared acted like he didn't even hear her and continued to trace his fingertips across her skin. "You have another condom?"

Penny was flabbergasted! No one ever asked her to do it a second time! "Yea, why?"

"Cause I can't get enough of you," Jared softly confessed.

THAT WAS the last night they saw.

At dawn the next morning, she had seen him sitting on the edge of her bed looking terribly worried.

He sat with a pen and a sticky note while she pretended to be asleep, watching him from squinting eyes. When he was done, he left the note on her jacket and left quietly.

It was painful to watch. They had been so in love the previous night and there he was sneaking away as if she was merely a one night stand.

What were you expecting? Didn't you beg for just once? She wasn't sure whether or not their encounter was her consolation, or condemnation. A part of her wished she had asked for more, perhaps if she had asked him to stay, maybe he would have?

Looking over at the note, she slowly got out of bed and then walked over to it. It seemed like a poem, Jared had employed his hidden talent at the eleventh hour, perhaps he thought that would make her understand.

I hate the sun and its scorch
I hate the rain messing up my porch
I hate the moon and the stars
I hate the powers that are not mine

I hate the ones I can't keep
I hate the things I can't control
Worse, I hate that you have become one of those.

When she was done reading it, tears had already welled up in her eyes and in one blink they came out in a rush for freedom.

She understood he may have been feeling a whole bunch of emotions than he was used to. She understood that he felt more love than he could fathom. The only reason why he hated her was that he was scared of loving beyond his control. So she decided that it was okay and that she was going to wait for him, for however long it may take she was going to be there … waiting.

DAYS WENT by and they didn't meet, no calls, no visits.

Until the Day of Doom…

Doomsday…

The Redbirds were scheduled to leave on a month long road trip. Hitting Texas, California, Arizona and then finally up to Washington State.

All groupies knew in order to continue following the band, *er,* the baseball team, you had to become a traveller as well. Follow them to where ever they ended up. Was she up for that? Was her heart up for another rejection?

No, she concluded.

She had determined that her infatuation with Owen Badwell was just that, a crush, a fantasy—and when the reality finally hit, the love she had felt wasn't real, it was just feelings of being wanted.

But Jared was different.

She had fallen in love with him—and for some weird reason, she felt he felt the same. But did he really? His absence told her otherwise. Maybe he was saving her from future harm, that he would end up hurting her in the end by sleeping with someone else anyways—was that it?

Maybe she was just a groupie after all—at hit and run.

Chapter Ten

"Dennis says they leave within the hour, you have enough gas in your car, Maria?" Nicole asked, quickly packing her suitcase.

Penny watched the two girls flying from one end of the apartment to the other. Her heart slowly breaking.

"Filled the tank last night," Maria replied, throwing her clothes into a duffle bag.

Nicole raised her eyes towards Penny just sitting immobile, stone-faced. "Where's your suitcase, you coming?"

Penny contemplated not to. Her heart was tugging at her though to move. "I don't think so."

The two girls halted their packing.

"Why not? You usually can't wait to get outta

Dodge," Maria snickered, placing her hands on her hips.

Penny nodded her head. "I know, only this time, I feel like…"

"Like what?" Nicole asked now, pulling her blond hair back into a ponytail.

"Like crying," Penny confessed.

The two girls shot looks at one another. Rolled their eyes.

"He wrote you a goodbye note, right? At least he was decent enough to do that. It was a one night stand, Pen. A hit and run, we've all been through it," Maria said, trying to convince Penny to come with them.

"Dennis told me that Jared's been super quiet these past few days," Nicole added, trying to alleviate the strain.

Penny looked at Nicole with wide eyes. "Do you think he's expecting me to follow him?"

Nicole shrugged her shoulders, "I dunno, anything's possible. But I don't want to see you get hurt again like last time. You've gotta stop falling head over heels for these guys."

Penny shook her head, "Like you? Are you head over heels for Dennis?"

Nicole shut her open mouth.

Maria grinned, "Look, it happens, we all move on. It's how we play the game. It's the thrill of the catch, remember?"

"Catch and release? A groupie's motto?" Nicole added.

Then Maria quickly looked at the front door. "Was that the door? Did someone just knock?"

The threesome all scurried into the living room. And when Nicole opened the door, she nearly passed out.

It was Jared Somner. Dressed in his casuals, alone—with no Dennis or Marco in sight.

"Hey Maria, is Penny here?"

Maria grinned, and then opened the door wider to expose both Nicole and Penny standing just behind it.

Jared didn't look at Penny but rather zoomed in on Nicole first. "Um, Dennis has moved on Nicole. He's asked that you not travel this time around, he doesn't want any distractions."

Nicole was devastated and crossed her arms across her chest. "And why didn't he come to tell me this himself?"

Jared shuffled his stance, "He's a coward that's why, and an idiot."

Nicole bit down on her lower lip and went to sit down on the couch to pout.

Then Jared finally rested eyes on Penny. She had been crying, he could tell. "Can I come in?"

Maria shook her head, "Yea, of course."

Jared walked in and then slowly walked over to Penny. So many emotions swelled within his heart, he didn't know where to start! "Can I speak to Penny alone?"

Penny was fuming inside! She knew damn well that Jared *wasn't* a coward! How dare he come in person to ask her to not follow him as well! "No," she quickly spat out, "I want them to hear what you have to say. We *all* need to hear what you're about to say."

Jared let go a cocky grin. "They don't need to hear this."

Penny crossed her arms across her chest in a protective stance. "You can't do this all the time!" She shouted back at him. "Sleep with us, spend time with us, and then ask us to just disappear!"

Jared gazed over at the two girls now sitting on the couch next to one another. They looked hurt, wounded. "What I want to say to you is private," he said, swallowing his pride.

Penny fought back her tears, she wasn't going to

allow him to see her cry. She wasn't going to give him the satisfaction. "No."

"No?"

Penny shook her head. "No."

"Penny…"

"No Jared, say what you have to say…"

Jared let go haughty smile, "Penny…"

Penny desperately tried to keep it all in, but tears swarmed her eyes. "What…?"

Jared soaked in her sadness and was about to fall to his knees. Keeping his composure, he gazed lovingly into her eyes, "Do you wanna meet my mom?"

THE END

Acknowledgments

Memphis Redbirds
St. Louis Cardinals

Thank You for reading, "Pop Fly Kiss" - An Alpha Male Curvy Woman Romance

If you liked this book, please leave a *positive* book review

BEST-SELLER!

TAUNT ME

Jason Ryan just resumed work as the CEO of his late father's company after his old man got killed by a drunk black man. Under strict instruction from his father's will to work with the carefully selected employees on the team or stand being replaced, Jason feels he got the bad end of the deal especially when he has to deal with his infuriating black secretary.

Devoted secretary, Kyra Aston is nothing short of a perfectionist. Unfortunately, due to the death of her former boss, her path collides with that of his son who is a hard worker but hates black people. Working with him is a nightmare and she wants so much to leave.

Jason has it bad. Seeing Kyra for the first time stirred up something in him. At first, he thought it was hatred, but when he discovers his feelings are close to the opposite, he is already far into her.

Soon, the shots they take at each other starts building a fire of sexual tension and Jason, knowing getting into a relationship with Kyra would affect his peace of mind and probably the business, he can't seem to keep his hands off her.

Their relationship soon becomes one built on lust and hatred for one another. Will Kyra fall in love with her racist boss and will Jason be able to look past her skin color?

BEST-SELLER!

Find out what happens to Kyra and Jason in this
hot BWWM Romance!

You Might Also Like

Mystique

When Becca Jones has a flat tire, she receives help from none other than her obnoxious white neighbor. He's charming, he's handsome, but Becca doesn't take the bait.

Aiden Holmsted is a millionaire tech wizard who has a crush on the dark beauty. But she's standoffish, mysterious and doesn't accept his help right away.

Unforeseen coincidences continually push them together until sparks fly and the mystery, clears.

Find humor and love with Becca and Aiden

in this

BWWM Romance!

Read Next

KISSER

Dr. Dexter Brody was a very successful dentist and was something of a ladies man. Owning one of the most thriving dental clinics in NYC, he wasn't short of female attention. But all the women he met lately were dull, boring and ordinary, until he meets Tia Michaels.

Tia the beautiful, black patient of his was unlike anyone he has ever met before, and she's even more captivating when his regular charms don't work so well on her.

Read what happens to Dexter and Tia in this HOT new BWWM Romance!

Coming Soon!

When Carson Avery stumbles upon the whereabouts of Tiffany Sales, the recluse lead singer of a forgotten girl group—he had to interview her.

Tanya Sommers—aka, *Tiffany Sales*—had changed her name years back, how did this nerdish white male reporter—from that online global music blog, **Lightening Bolt**—find her? She had been hiding out for the past fifteen years—why does he want an interview *now*?

After their meeting and the interview is over, Carson not only finds a great story for his blog, but he's found his soul mate.

Online Retailers:

Amazon, Barnes & Noble, Kobo and Apple Books
ebook & paperback

About the Author

Savannah Kole is an emerging author of Romance and Contemporary Modern Fiction. Savannah has a wide range of writing interests and is currently living the incognito digital lifestyle.

Savannah is publishing books for your personal enjoyment only, especially if you like: Black Women White Male Romance, Alpha Male Curvy Women Romance, and short story series.

Also by Savannah Kole

BWWM ROMANCE

Mystique

Kisser

Taunt Me

Sing Me a Song

ALPHA MALE CURVY WOMAN ROMANCE

Meet Me on Social Media

The Butterfly

Pop Fly Kiss

STANDALONES

Love & Loss

Other Books Published by Ardent Artist
Books Pen Authors

Emma DaSilva

The Demon Princess

Spellcasters - The Wizards of Roseburn

Harper Grast

A Werewolf's Heart

Raelynn Faith

Sweet Treats

ZT Oser

Kenyan Sunset

Ardent Artist Books Limited Series Comics

Curse of the Sapphire - Issues 1-6

Other Books Published by Ardent Artist Books Pen Authors

www.ingramcontent.com/pod-product-compliance
Lightning Source LLC
Chambersburg PA
CBHW072110150726
47999CB00005B/1982